WELCOME

Beast Quest

Collect the special coins in this book.
You will earn one gold coin for
every chapter you read.

Once you have finished all the chapters,
find out what to do with your gold coins at
the back of the book.

With special thanks to Allan Frewin Jones

To Nathaneal and Josiah Green

www.beastquest.co.uk

ORCHARD BOOKS

First published in Great Britain in 2016 by The Watts Publishing Group

1 3 5 7 9 10 8 6 4 2

Text © 2016 Beast Quest Limited.
Cover illustrations by Steve Sims © Beast Quest Limited 2016
Inside illustrations by Raúl Horacio Vila (Beehive Illustration) © Beast Quest Limited 2016

Beast Quest is a registered trademark of Beast Quest Limited
Series created by Beast Quest Limited, London

A CIP catalogue record for this book is available from the British Library.

ISBN 978 1 40834 084 4

Printed and bound by CPI Group (UK) Ltd, Croydon, CR0 4YY

MIX
Paper from
responsible sources
FSC® C104740

The paper and board used in this book are made from wood from responsible sources

Orchard Books
An imprint of Hachette Children's Group
Part of The Watts Publishing Group Limited
Carmelite House, 50 Victoria Embankment, London EC4Y 0DZ

An Hachette UK Company
www.hachette.co.uk
www.hachettechildrens.co.uk

SAUREX
THE SILENT CREEPER

BY ADAM BLADE

ORCHARD

GWILDOR
BORDERLANDS

MUDDY LAKE

MANGROVE
SWAMP

DUNES

DESERT

CONTENTS

Do you know the worst thing about so-called heroes? They just don't give up.

Well, villains can be just as stubborn… That pesky boy, Tom, and his lackey, Elenna, may have thwarted our siege of Jengtor, but the battle is not over. There are other prizes to be found throughout my kingdom!

In Gwildor's borderlands lie the four pieces of the Broken Star, a legendary "gift" that fell from the sky many, many years ago. Each piece gives its holder immense power, and whoever brings all four pieces together will be undefeatable!

To obtain each piece, one must find a way past the Beasts which guard them. Kensa and I have tricks up our sleeves – and a head-start on our enemies. With the star in our hands, no one will stop us from reclaiming Gwildor.

And then? Avantia!

Your future ruler,

Emperor Jeng

THE ENEMIES ESCAPE

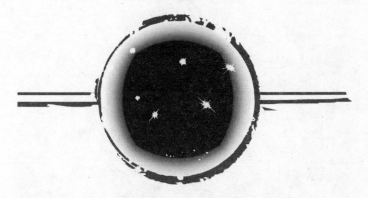

"Kensa and Jeng have escaped!" Tom stared into the mud hut where his two enemies had been imprisoned.

"But the doorway was guarded!" cried Tyroll, the tall elder of the village.

Elenna stood at his side, grim-

faced. "Kensa must have used her
magic to get them free," she said.

As she spoke, a man came bustling
up. "Two camels have been stolen
from the stables!" he said with
a gasp.

Tom and Elenna exchanged a knowing glance.

"The witch and the treacherous emperor must have taken them," said Tom. "They can't have gone far." He strode from the hut. "We'll follow them. May we take a pair of camels?"

"Of course," said Tyroll. "But you fought long and hard against Okko the Sand Monster. You cannot leave without eating first."

Tom frowned. They were running out of time on this Quest, and despair was gnawing at his heart.

Their journey across the realm of Gwildor had been gruelling – but they had fought off Beasts of ice and smoke and sand, winning three of the four shards of the Broken Star.

Irina, the kingdom's Good Witch
had told them the legend of the star.
Known by the people as the "gift from
the sky", it had fallen to the ground in
Gwildor long ago, shattering into four
shards of immense power. The ancient
tales told that the star fragments
could control the weather – creating
terrible storms, choking fog or icy
winds. So a Good Witch named Clara
had taken the fragments to remote
corners of Gwildor, so that no villain
would ever be able to wield their
power. Guarded by ferocious Beasts,
these fragments had lain hidden for
so long that many folk had ceased
believing in them.

But two people knew the legends were true: Jeng, Gwildor's wicked emperor, and the witch Kensa. They were determined to gather the fragments and use them for their wicked purposes.

Tom's battle with Okko had been fierce and savage. He could still feel the ache where his broken leg had been healed by the power of Skor's green jewel.

I can't let pain and weariness stop me. Kensa and Jeng will use all their terrible powers to find the fourth shard of the star.

And Tom knew that even a single star fragment could do great damage in the wrong hands.

A fire had been kindled in the middle of the village. Already the chill of night was sweeping in, and many of the villagers were huddled around the flames, reaching out grateful hands to the warmth.

Tom stared around the village – the simple mud huts had been smashed in his battle with Okko.

"Eat with us," Tyroll asked again. "You saved us from certain death."

"Thank you, but we can't spare the time," Tom said sadly. A weight settled in his heart as he thought of the expanse of empty desert that surrounded this remote oasis. "Which way should we go?"

"Might the star fragments guide

us?" Elenna asked.

Tom took the three crystals from his pouch and laid them on the ground. He stared down at them, willing them to give him some clue.

Nothing happened.

Tom screwed his eyes shut, desperately trying to come up with a plan to continue the Quest.

"Tom, look!" cried Elenna. He opened his eyes and saw that two of the shards were trembling in the sand, shifting towards one another.

"Those are the pieces from Gryph and Thoron," Tom said, as the two shards suddenly leaped together and fused. The third piece began to quiver too.

Tom snatched it up. "Remember what Irina told us?" he said to Elenna. "If the star joins together again it will become a deadly weapon. Even three parts could be dangerous." He pushed the third fragment into his pouch and picked up the two fused shards, handing them to Elenna. "Keep them somewhere safe."

"Tyroll!" Anxious voices cried out from near the fire. "Something strange is happening! Bad magic!"

Tom spun around, his hand already on his sword hilt.

He saw that people were backing away from one section of the roaring fire.

"The flames have changed colour," said Elenna as they ran forwards. In one corner of the bonfire the flames had become a curious shade of purple. "What can that mean?"

Is this Kensa's magic?

"Stay back!" Tom cried to the crowd.

But then a familiar face appeared in the flickering flames.

"It's Irina!" Tom raised his arms.
"Don't be afraid," he called to the
people.

"I have little time," Irina's voice
rose above the crackling fire. "The

fourth Beast you seek is Saurex. He is a lizard, a chameleon of great size – and he is the most deadly of the four!"

"How do we find him?" Tom asked.

"Look to the stars," Irina said. The flames guttered and spat. The face of the Good Witch melted away.

"Irina!" Tom called, staring anxiously into the fire. But she was gone. He looked at Elenna. "I'm sure she meant to tell us more."

Elenna was gazing up into the sky. She thrust her arm out, her finger pointing to a distant constellation. "Does that look like a lizard to you?" she asked.

Tom followed the line of her finger. Low on the horizon, a long cluster of

stars hung over the black hills – and
Elenna was right, they did seem to
form the outline of a crouching lizard.

He turned to Tyroll. "That is our
way ahead."

Tyroll looked anxious. "The
Poisoned Swamp lies in that
direction. It is a deadly place!"

"We must go where our Quest

leads us," Tom insisted.

"Then may good fortune guard you on your way," Tyroll said, and sighed.

Within a few moments, Tom and Elenna were mounted on borrowed camels, bidding the villagers farewell and setting off on the last journey of their Quest.

Tom shifted his weight in the high saddle, getting used to the camel's long, rocking stride. The cool desert air wafted over them as they headed deeper into the desert night.

There's something ominous about that constellation, Tom thought as he stared towards the horizon. *It feels as though we're being lured into terrible danger.*

DEADLY PURSUIT

Tom's head was bowed with worry as he rode through the night. His battles to win the first three shards of the Broken Star had been gruelling – but Irina had said the next Beast would be the most deadly.

Elenna's voice broke into his gloomy thoughts. "Camels are hard to ride," she said. "The way they move makes me feel seasick."

Tom lifted his head and nodded. He was gradually adjusting to the roll and sway of the tall animal beneath him, but being perched on the hump of this strange creature still made him feel awkward and vulnerable.

"Horses are so much quicker, too," he added.

A sudden urgency filled Elenna's voice. "What's that?"

Tom peered into the distance. A band of white light stretched along the flat horizon and the sky was tinged with blue. Day was coming.

Two far-off shapes were silhouetted against the growing light.

"Kensa and Jeng!" said Tom, instantly alert. He dug his heels into his camel's flanks and it broke into a lurching trot.

They clung on as the camels closed in on the humped shapes. Tom's hopes of catching up with their enemies were quickly dashed. Tethered to a rock in front of them were two more camels.

"Kensa and Jeng must have left them here," said Elenna.

Tom pulled on the reins of his own camel, approaching cautiously.

He glanced over his shoulder. "It may be a trap," he said.

Elenna nodded, her face watchful.

Tom urged his mount on, standing

in the stirrups and leaning forwards. He saw that the two animals were standing on the brink of a great, plunging chasm, from which an unpleasant, rotting smell wafted up.

"What's that horrible stink?"

Elenna said with a gasp.

Tom dismounted and walked to the edge. The drop was giddy-making, and the land below was startlingly different from the desert. The stench of mould and decay was thick in his nose. He retched and turned away as

bile rose in his throat. He had never smelled anything so disgusting.

"I think we've found the Poisoned Swamp," he said grimly.

The foul swamp stretched away to the horizon, a heavy, greenish mist swirling among twisted trees and crawling creepers. The place looked diseased. And sweeping in across the sky were mountains of dark cloud, ragged with falling rain.

"I can see why it's avoided," Tom murmured, swallowing hard as his stomach heaved. He leaned over the jagged edge, seeking a way down.

"We'll never get the camels down there," said Elenna, joining him at the edge. "If I set the other two free, perhaps they'll all head back to the oasis?"

They untied the two camels. "Go!" Tom cried, waving his arms. "Find water – go home!"

The camels trotted off. They would be fine – and the villagers would be grateful to see them again.

"Is there a pathway down?" asked Elenna.

Tom pointed to a crumbling lip of rock that ran steeply down the cliff. "That looks like a possibility," he said.

Tom lowered himself over the cliff edge. Keeping his back to the rock face, he sidled down, testing every step before moving on.

"It's solid," he called up.

Elenna joined him on the sheer cliff.

They edged along, clinging to fissures in the rock. Halfway down the cliff, the path was split open by a deep crack.

"Brace yourself against the sides," said Tom.

He straddled the cleft, finding ridges as he lowered himself down the path. He looked up – Elenna was following, her face intent.

Tom came to a place where the cliff leaned back and was broken into long, sloping steps.

"It's easier here," he told Elenna.

Moments after he had spoken, he

felt the first flecks of cold rain on his face. He waited for Elenna to join him, but by then the rain was falling steadily.

"It's getting very slippery

underfoot," Elenna said.

"We'll have to watch every step," Tom agreed. A fall from this height would be disastrous.

Shoulder to shoulder, they edged down, the slope beneath their feet becoming slick with rushing rivulets of brown water. Tom's foot slid and he lost balance. He felt Elenna's hand snatch at his collar and jerk him back from the edge.

"Thanks," he gasped, steadying himself against the slithery rock.

A moment later, the entire section of rock underneath Elenna gave way.

She cried out as she plunged downwards. Tom caught her hand, but the ground under him was washing away as well. A flood of muddy water sluiced down over him, sending him tumbling down. He saw the green fog swallow Elenna, and a few moments later he heard a yelp and a splash.

He plunged into the stifling fog, landing in deep sludge.

Tom lay panting in the stinking ooze. It was disgusting – but at least he was alive.

"Are you all right?" Elenna rose to her feet, dripping slime.

"I think so." Tom lifted himself from the sucking mud.

Elenna pinched her nose. "The stink is much worse now!"

"It'll choke us if we don't do

something about it," agreed Tom. He tore a dry strip from the hem of his tunic and tied it around his mouth and nose to keep out the worst of the poisonous stench.

Elenna did the same, and then

they helped one another out of
the deep mud. Tom searched for
higher ground, peering through the
hanging curtains of green mist at
the deformed and knotted trees that
surrounded them, their crooked
branches hanging with ugly, tangled
vines.

"Kensa and Jeng must have come
this way," he said.

"Even with Kensa's magic, they
wouldn't be able to move quickly
through these trees," said Elenna.
"Ugh!" She shuddered as a long,
slime-dripping vine crawled over her
shoulder.

They waded on through knee-deep
water crusted with green scum.

Suddenly Tom's mind was filled with a dark, sinister hatred. The red jewel of Torgor was warning him of the presence of a Beast. "There's something dangerous up ahead," he murmured. "I can feel it."

Tom felt a sharp pinch of discomfort on his arm. He winced, feeling the pain swell. Something had stung him.

"Tom!" Elenna's face was filled with revulsion. A fat black leech was clinging to his forearm, its mouth already sucking greedily at his blood.

He drew his sword and flicked the leech off with its tip, leaving a ring of red bite marks. "We need to get out of the water," he said. "The swamp must be full of these things!"

Shuddering, Elenna followed Tom to a huge mangrove tree, its roots lifting high out of the slime, its branches spreading up into the green canopy of mist.

Tom heaved himself out of the clinging mire, clambering up the hooked roots and finding a place where the sprawling branches opened out. The tree was slick with rain, but he managed to get a firm footing before leaning down to help up Elenna.

He had hoisted her halfway when he saw a flicker of movement. Before he could react, a slender blue ribbon came lashing out of the mist.

Elenna gave a cry as the whip-like thread wrapped itself around her waist.

It was a tongue!

"Elenna!" Tom cried, as his friend was ripped from his grasp. He caught

a final glimpse of her frightened face before she vanished into the maze of branches and vines.

"Elenna!" he shouted again.

But all he could hear was the rustle of the branches and the endless drip of water from the leaves.

3

OVERPOWERED!

Tom leapt from the tree, grasping a hanging vine and swinging himself up onto a high branch. Balancing himself, he lunged forwards, jumping from limb to limb.

The swamp was a tangle of dangling creepers and whip-thin branches. Tom swung on a thick tendril, staring ahead, following a trail of broken vines and cracked tree limbs.

He could hear Elenna's voice calling through the fog.

"Tom! This way!"

He spun around a high horizontal branch, releasing his grip to fly through the trees. But his foot got tangled in a creeper and he was brought to a bone-jarring halt in the crack where a trunk divided. Winded, he lifted his head, listening intently.

Elenna? Where are you?

He clambered to his feet. The swamp was horribly still, the quiet broken only by the creak of branches and the sucking sounds of the thick mud.

Tom put his hand to the red jewel,

focusing his mind. A low, sinister voice filled his head.

Who dares enter the realm of Saurex?

The menace in the voice chilled Tom's blood. He drew his sword, bracing himself for an attack. The mist hung in dense curtains. Trees jutted through it like deformed limbs holding slimy vines.

The mist stirred and Tom saw a flicker of movement.

"Saurex?" he whispered. He gripped his sword, every sinew tensing.

A figure emerged from the swirl of green mist.

"Kensa!"

The witch's wet hair hung over her forehead, her clothes dripping mud as she stepped out onto a horizontal branch. One hand clutched her deadly Lightning Staff. She looked at Tom with a haughty, mocking glint in her eyes.

"I see you're all alone," she sneered. "Has your friend abandoned you? I don't blame her – you must be a terribly boring companion."

Tom gritted his teeth, ignoring the witch's taunts as he walked along the branch towards her, his sword ready in his hand.

Kensa's eyes glinted with malice as she aimed the point of her

Lightning Staff at his chest.

"You seem to be all alone, as well," Tom said, as he closed in on her. "Where's Jeng? Did he get sick of you?"

"Oh – he's not so far away," Kensa replied scornfully. "In fact…" Her eyes darted upwards. Tom glanced up in time to see a pair of heavy boots hurtling down towards him. "Here he comes now!"

Jeng clung to a vine as he came plunging down. Tom caught a glimpse of wild, savage eyes.

Tom raised his shield to fend off the attack, but Jeng's weight was too much for him. The boots struck his shield with a dull thud, sending pain shooting through his arm and shoulder, overbalancing him. He slithered from branch to branch. Knocked breathless by the long fall, Tom plunged into deep water,

choking as the foul stuff filled his
mouth and nose.

Angry at being caught out so easily,
Tom rose to his feet, coughing to

clear his lungs. He held his shield firm and his sword poised, ready to do battle.

He stared up. Where was Jeng?

Something hit him hard behind the knees, tipping him over. Filthy water closed over his face again. He rose, gasping for breath.

Jeng was right there, standing knee-deep in the swirling water.

Tom doubled up as a savage punch drove into his ribs. A kick to his wrist sent his sword cartwheeling through the air, stabbing point-down into a hummock of grass. Biting back his cry of pain, Tom scrambled towards it, but his shoulders were caught in a vice-like grip. Powerful arms pushed him face-first into the watery mud.

The foul sludge filled his mouth and nose once more, blinding him and clogging his ears.

After a moment, Tom's head was dragged up out of the water.

"Give me the pieces of the star!" Jeng snarled.

"Never!" Tom gasped.

He managed to snatch a breath as the arms pushed him under the water again, a knee digging between his shoulder blades.

Tom struggled, fighting against Jeng's strength. But his feet couldn't get purchase in the thick, sucking mud, and Jeng's whole weight was bearing down on him.

His head was dragged from the water again.

"Give me the star fragments!" Jeng bellowed.

"No!" Tom panted, mud clogging his eyes and nose.

"Then you'll drown!" roared Jeng. Tom felt the fingers on the back of his neck tighten. He took a breath.

"Really, Jeng, you're such a clod sometimes." Kensa's mocking voice rang in Tom's ears. "We need more than brute force to deal with him."

Coughing, Tom hung in Jeng's grip, sucking in air, gathering his strength for a final attempt to free himself.

"What have we here?" cried Kensa.

Tom writhed in Jeng's hands as the witch ripped away his shoulder pouch.

No! The shard!

Kensa shoved her hand into the pouch and drew out the shard of the

Broken Star. Her look of gloating triumph faded. "Only one piece!" she snarled. "His scrawny sidekick must have the rest."

Kensa's cruel face came close to Tom's. "Where is she?" she snarled, the point of her Lightning Staff aimed at his forehead. "Tell me quick, or I'll let Jeng dunk your head until your lungs fill with slime!"

"She was taken by Saurex," Tom gasped. "I was following her." He was thinking fast now. "I know which way they went – if you kill me, you'll never find them!"

"We'll get the truth from you!" snarled Jeng.

"I'll never tell," shouted Tom.

"We need to work together if we're going to find her." He coughed again. "I've heard the Beast in my mind – he's more powerful than you can imagine. Kill me, and Saurex will destroy you!"

Gripping Tom's neck with one hand, Jeng drew a long, curved dagger. "We'll finish you, then we'll deal with the Beast!" he growled.

Kensa caught Jeng's raised arm. "Let's not do anything rash," she said. "I know this boy – if we keep him alive, he'll fight like a fury to save his precious companion." Her voice slithered like a snake. "While he's saving his friend, we can swipe the other fragments of the star...

Everyone wins."

Jeng's fingers loosened and Tom was able to get to his feet, panting hard, dripping with marsh water.

Kensa aimed the end of her Lightning Staff into his face. "We have a truce for the moment," she said. "But if you make one wrong move, you won't need to worry about Jeng." Her eyes flashed. "*I'll* be the one to kill you!'

4

THE UNSEEN BEAST

Tom's two captors pushed him roughly through the swamp – avoiding the deeper water as much as possible. He knew he could call on the power of his golden breastplate to break free of the rope they'd tied around his wrists, but he had no sword – and Kensa wouldn't hesitate to use her Lightning Staff on him.

I must wait for a better chance.

"What do you know about the Beast?" demanded Kensa, poking him in the back with her Lightning Staff.

Tom glared around at her. "It's some kind of lizard," he said. "Like a chameleon – it's able to change colour so it can camouflage itself." He remembered the menacing voice in his head. "And it hates intruders."

"Enough of this," muttered Jeng. "We will kill the Beast easily enough." He stared into Tom's face. "Tell me," he said eagerly. "What is Avantia like? I must know more about it for when I become emperor of Avantia *and* Gwildor."

"You'll never rule those realms," said Tom grimly. "Not while I have blood in my veins."

Jeng grinned savagely. "I'll let your blood out soon enough," he said. "And when the Broken Star is repaired, I'll have all the power I need."

"When we have all the pieces," Kensa broke in sharply, "*we* will rule those realms. Together."

Jeng frowned at the witch. "That's what I meant."

"I think King Hugo and Queen Aroha will have something to say about that," Tom said.

Jeng thumped his chest with a clenched fist. "Aroha will be *my* queen once I've dealt with that thief, Hugo," he said.

Tom ducked under a hanging branch, hating the wet slither of dangling vines on his face. "In what way is King Hugo a thief?" he asked, a small smile curling his lip as he saw Kensa's fight for balance after her boot plunged into thick mud.

"Aroha was meant to marry me," Jeng growled. "That wastrel Hugo stole her away."

"That's not true," Tom retorted, remembering the joy of the wedding ceremony. "King Hugo and Queen Aroha have been in love for years."

"Call me a liar, would you?" Jeng let out a roar of fury and aimed a punch. Tom jerked back just in time to avoid the blow. "Love has nothing to do with it!" Jeng raged, raising his fist for another blow.

Kensa grabbed his arm. "All in good time," she said, dragging him back. "Knock him unconscious now and we may never find Saurex."

Jeng pointed a finger at Tom, his face red with fury. "Punishment is only postponed," he snarled. "But call me a liar again, and I'll give you reason to fear me."

"I doubt that," said Tom, glowering at him.

Spittle flew from Jeng's mouth as he raved. "Aroha was promised to *me*," he said, his eyes blazing. "We were to be married so that her kingdom of Tangala would be united with my realm of Gwildor."

Tom wiped a dribble of spit off his cheek with his tied hands. He understood why such an arrangement would suit Jeng – it would allow him to attack

Avantia on two fronts.

He was about to put this to the enraged emperor when he caught a glimpse of something through the trees, only a little way off – a pale shape lying in a bed of broken ferns...

Elenna!

"What have you seen?" snapped Kensa. "Ahhh! The girl!" She peered through the trees. "She is lying very still," she said. "Perhaps Saurex killed her."

Tom glared at the witch, loathing the indifference in her voice.

"Hold the boy back," Kensa said. "I'll get the star fragments."

Tom stared intently at Elenna, desperate for any sign of life. *She*

can't be dead! His heart pushed up
into his throat. It wasn't possible.

Jeng's hands came down heavily on
Tom's shoulders, pinning him in place
as Kensa shoved her way through
branches and vines.

Tom watched helplessly as the witch
stooped over Elenna and loosened
the strap of her shoulder pouch. She
thrust her hand inside.

"I have them!" she shouted, standing
up and turning to Tom and Jeng, her
hand raised above her head, the joined
fragments of the star in her fist.

Tom strained to free his hands. If
Elenna was hurt he had to get to her –
he had to help her. He couldn't let it
end like this!

"Be still or I'll drown you like a
kitten," snarled Jeng, his fingers like
metal clamps on Tom's shoulders.

"Take the star fragments," Tom

cried. "Just let me help Elenna."

"Be silent, boy!" growled Jeng.

Then Tom noticed a small movement in the ferns.

A huge shape suddenly became clear in his eyes. A giant lizard, its scaly body dappled with a thousand shades of green and brown – so perfectly camouflaged among the ferns that it had been virtually invisible until it turned its head on its long neck and its blue tongue flickered between sharp fangs.

Saurex loomed over Elenna and Kensa.

A moment later, a long, whipping tail swung out, looping around Kensa's legs and lifting her screaming into the air.

The star fragments fell from her hand as she writhed in the Beast's grip.

Tom held his hands up to Jeng.
"Free me!" he gasped. "We'll fight
Saurex together!"

"You take me for a fool, boy?"
growled Jeng, watching the Beast
with fearful eyes.

"Then use the fragment of the
star you took from me!" cried
Tom. "Otherwise, Saurex will kill
them both!"

Saurex was shaking Kensa like a
rabbit, and one of the Beast's clawed
feet was poised above Elenna, as
though about to stamp down on her.

"Use the fragment?" Jeng took
the star fragment from the pouch
and held it up, his other hand still
gripping Tom's neck. "What do you

mean, boy? I don't know how to use the fragment."

Tom stared at him.

There was no time to explain the power of the shard to Jeng. The Beast was about to crush Elenna – in moments, she would be dead.

BATTLE IN THE SWAMP

Tom wrenched free of Jeng's grip, turned and kicked high, knocking the star fragment out of Jeng's fingers. Then he thrust his shoulder into the emperor's stomach, sending him staggering backwards.

Tom leaped sideways, rolled across the slimy grass and caught the falling crystal between his tied hands. The Beast loomed menacingly over Elenna, Kensa still dangling helplessly from his coiled tail.

Tom sprang up, pointing the fragment at Saurex. Instantly, he felt the power of Okko pulse

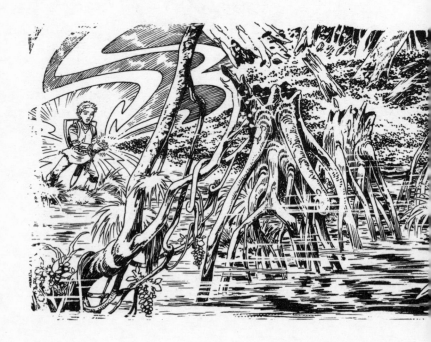

through the crystal, sand gushing from the tip and forming a fist, which punched through the trees, smashing branches and vines aside as it struck Saurex, driving him backwards.

The sand stuck to his scaly body

and flew into his eyes. The Beast roared, a high, terrible sound.

Kensa writhed in the grip of the sinuous tail, aiming her Lightning Staff. A bolt of fire burned the coils that held her feet, releasing her so that she crashed down into the ferns.

With all that sand on his body, Saurex won't be able to camouflage himself for a while! Tom thought as he flung himself through the trees and waded to where Elenna lay.

Saurex's cries echoed through the swamp as he blundered away. Blinded by sand, the Beast was retreating – but Tom knew their respite would only be temporary.

He dropped to his knees at Elenna's side.

Is she even alive?

Elenna let out a long, shuddering breath. Tom felt a rush of relief as her eyes opened blearily.

"What happened?" she gasped.

"Saurex took you – I've driven him off." Tom raised his bound hands. Calling on the power of the golden breastplate, he flexed his muscles and snapped the rope.

He helped Elenna to her feet and they stood back to back, ready to fight.

"Be careful," Tom said. "Kensa and Jeng are close by." He frowned. Where were they? Kensa had fallen into deep ferns, but now there was no sign of her. He looked over his shoulder – Jeng was also gone.

"I need to find my sword," Tom said. "Wait here – call if you see anything."

He waded through the clinging mud. The sword had fallen somewhere nearby. He wiped mud out of his eyes, aware that he was coated in the greenish slime. It stank, but he tried to ignore it – he had to find his sword.

He saw a silvery glint among the arched roots of a tree.

That's it!

He had almost reached his weapon when he heard something crashing through the branches. *Saurex!* The huge Beast was hurtling towards Tom, his head thrust forward on a long neck, claws ripping tree limbs and creepers aside.

The Beast was still half covered in sand, but his eyes were clear again and there was a vengeful light in them that froze Tom's blood.

He heard the Beast's voice in his head. *Where are you, puny boy? All who trespass on my swamp must face the consequences!*

Tom froze as Saurex towered over him.

No sword! How do I fight?

But to Tom's astonishment, the great Beast stormed right past him, his burning gaze searching left and right. And there – high on his head, nestled among a row of deadly spikes – Tom saw the fourth fragment of the Broken Star.

Saurex blundered on, hissing and snarling.

How did he not see me?

Then Tom realised he was mired from head to foot in mud. *Now* I'm *camouflaged!*

He watched in relief as the huge lizard stamped away through the swamp, leaving a trail of destruction.

Tom ran to his sword, new hope entering him as his fingers closed around the hilt.

He heard Saurex roar.

Had the Beast seen Elenna?

"No!" Tom gasped. He plunged through the marsh, summoning the might of his golden leg armour to give him the extra speed he needed. Mud sprayed high as he ran, desperate to get to Elenna before Saurex attacked.

The Beast reared up, tongue flickering, fangs and claws gleaming. Elenna was a tiny, brave figure in his shadow, arrow to bow, her face determined.

Tom snatched at Saurex's whipping tail, clinging on, using it to swing up onto the Beast's high back. He used the spikes that jutted from the ridged spine as stepping stones.

The Beast's body twisted as he

turned his head, snapping his jaws
at Tom. Sand crumbled away from
the thrashing body as Saurex reared
up, trying to throw Tom clear. But he
was on the Beast's shoulders already,

sure-footed, keeping his balance as the silent creeper bucked and reared.

Tom lunged upwards, his hand closing around the star shard lodged high on Saurex's head. He jerked at it – but the fragment would not come loose, and his feet were slipping on the shiny scales. He tried to jab his sword under the crystal, but with a ferocious roar, Saurex shook him off.

Tom tumbled through the air, only just managing to keep hold of his sword. Soft mud broke his fall and he was on his feet again in an instant.

He swung his shield off his back, ready to fight for his life – but Saurex had vanished.

Where? How?

Of course – now the sand had fallen away from his body, the Beast had used his chameleon powers to camouflage himself again.

Elenna was standing among the ferns, her bow ready, an arrow nocked as she sought her target.

"It's no use," Tom called to her. "Cover yourself in mud so Saurex can't find you – I'll lure him away."

Elenna waded into the mud and lowered herself to the shoulders, finally dipping her head into the slime. She rose up, coated in the thick muck – not as completely invisible as Saurex, but camouflaged safely enough.

Tom pressed his hand against his belt, feeling Torgor's jewel under his palm.

Saurex? He projected his thoughts through the jewel, knowing that the Beast would hear him. *You hide well,* he taunted. *If only you fought as well, you'd be a formidable enemy.*

From the corner of his eye, Tom saw a large area of trunks, branches and hanging vines shift and blur. A huge outline emerged from the confusion of browns and greens and suddenly the giant lizard was right in front of him, towering up on its powerful hind legs, its mouth open as it roared, its tongue lashing out.

Tom lunged at the Beast's scaled

belly, stabbing upwards, his shield raised to ward off a ferocious swipe from a clawed arm. His sword rang on the armoured scales, his blow driving Saurex back. Tom darted between the huge legs, striking left and right, the force of his attack keeping the Beast off-balance.

Saurex swung his tail, almost cutting Tom's legs from under him as he leaped high. The tongue lashed down, forcing Tom to backflip to avoid it coiling around his sword arm. All the while the claws raked in from both sides, and the Beast's head darted at Tom, deadly fangs snapping.

I can't defeat Saurex like this.

Tom saw the branches of a tall tree
hanging over the Beast's head.

*If I can climb up there, maybe
I'll be able to cut the star fragment
free.* Once the crystal was no longer
embedded in Saurex's head, Tom was
sure the Beast would stop fighting.

He threw himself towards the
tree trunk, ducking as more blows
rained down from the swiping arms,
darting aside as the deadly tongue
lashed out.

He leaped high, grasping a jutting
branch. But as he heaved himself up,
he felt something wind around his
waist.

Saurex's tongue.

It tightened around Tom and

dragged him off the branch. He
managed to dig the fingers of one
hand into the cracked bark, swinging
wildly at the tongue with his sword.

Saurex's jaws opened wide as the

tongue dragged at Tom. His fingers were slipping. He stared in dismay over his shoulder. The Beast's great gaping maw filled his vision. Another moment and he'd be ripped loose and drawn in between those dagger-like fangs.

He'd be eaten alive!

6

A KNIFE TO THE THROAT

Just as Tom's fingers were about
to be torn loose from the branch,
he heard a sharp whizzing sound,
followed by a *thunk!* Then there was
a high-pitched screech of pain as
Saurex's grip around Tom's waist
slackened. He flicked a glance over
his shoulder and his spirits leapt at

the sight of what he saw.

One of Elenna's arrows had pierced the long tongue and pinned it to the trunk of the tree. Tom jammed the blade of his sword down between his waist and the tongue and gave a jerk. The tongue uncoiled and Tom dropped to the ground, landing feet-first, sword and shield ready.

"Thank you!" he called to Elenna, who had nocked another arrow.

Saurex was writhing in agony, his claws tearing at the tree as he tried to free his tongue.

Tom raised his sword.

"Saurex!" he called. "Submit, and I will free you."

With another screech, the Beast raised a clawed foot and stamped down at Tom. He skipped aside, then spun around and leaped onto the great leg, the edge of his sword pressing against Saurex's neck.

"Yield, and I will spare your life!"

Steam snorted from the Beast's nostrils, its wild eyes staring down at him. Then Saurex became still and his voice echoed in Tom's mind – no longer frenzied, but calm.

Worthy victor, it said. *I submit.*

Saurex lifted an arm to his head and clawed out the star fragment from among the spines. It tumbled through the air, glittering and shining. Tom caught it and pushed it into his tunic, wondering what power this fragment would have.

Tom climbed the tree and used his sword-tip to prise the arrow from Saurex's tongue. The Beast locked eyes with Tom for a moment and its voice echoed in his head.

You have my gratitude, Son of Gwildor.

Tom watched as Saurex turned and sped away through the trees, changing his colour to a dappled green that blended perfectly with the foliage.

Elenna lowered her bow, smiling as she joined Tom.

"We still only have two pieces of the star," he said, turning to gaze along the path of destruction left by the camouflaged Beast. "We need to get the other fragments back from Kensa and Jeng."

Elenna said nothing.

Puzzled, Tom turned to look at her.

His blood froze. Jeng held Elenna in a vicious grip, one hand over her mouth, the other holding a curved dagger to her throat. A trickle of blood ran down into her collar. Elenna's eyes were wide

with both fear and anger.

Kensa stepped out from behind
Jeng. "I knew you wouldn't let us
down," she sneered. "All your hard
work has served us very well." She
held out a greedy hand. "Give me
the shards."

Elenna tore Jeng's grip away from
her mouth. "Don't do it!" she cried.
"They mustn't win!"

Kensa's smile widened. "Well,
actually, we *must* win," she said.
"Otherwise you will pay the
ultimate price."

Tom pulled the two star fragments
from his tunic and tossed them
to Kensa. "Take them. Just let
Elenna go."

But Kensa didn't seem to hear him. She was holding the two crystals in her trembling hands, her lips twitching and her eyes gleaming with a mad greed. She pulled the two fused pieces of the star from her robe. Jeng watched intently as she brought all the fragments together. The shard of Okko and the fragment from Saurex trembled and jumped suddenly towards the other pieces.

"At last!" cried Kensa, as the four pieces locked together to form a jagged star. She thrust the artefact onto the tip of her Lightning Staff, her eyes filled with a wicked eagerness.

Tom's heart felt heavy in his chest.

At the very climax of the Quest, the witch had defeated him.

Kensa lifted the staff high. Tom saw pulses of white light throbbing in the star. "I feel it!" she cried. "The power of the Fallen Star is mine!"

"And what will you do now you have the power?" Tom asked.

"Watch and see," Kensa replied, lowering the staff and aiming it at a tree trunk.

She thrust her arm out. A lash of white flame spat from the star. Tom felt the heat on his face. Even Jeng winced. There was a burst of pale fire and the tree vanished, blasted to grey ash that drifted on the stifling air.

Grinning savagely, Kensa turned the staff on Tom. "Excellent," she crowed. "Now let's see what effect it has on living flesh!"

Tom lifted his chin, staring into Kensa's eyes, bracing himself for death.

"But, maybe not," said the witch, lowering the staff. "As satisfying as it would be to blast you to ash, it will be even more satisfying to make you watch your homeland be destroyed."

Tom set his jaw, fighting the despair that threatened to overwhelm him. He had failed at the last stage of his Quest. All his efforts to save Avantia and Gwildor had been in vain!

Kensa lifted the staff above her head, holding it horizontally, her wild eyes staring. "Through the power of my Lightning Staff we will travel to Avantia," she cried. She began to turn in a slow circle and, as she did so, a thread of red light spun out from the tip of the staff, forming a burning ring above her head.

She lowered the staff and the ring descended until its lower rim touched the ground.

She's opening a portal between kingdoms! Tom longed to fling himself at the witch, to cut her staff in two and drain her power – but while Jeng held a knife at Elenna's throat, he was powerless.

Just give me one chance.

The air shimmered inside the burning ring. There was a brief blur, then Tom saw the towers and walls

and turrets of King Hugo's palace.

Kensa had cut a doorway right through to Avantia.

"You have great skills, Kensa," growled Jeng. "But do not use your witchcraft on King Hugo." His eyes filled with malice and madness. "I will settle my score with him in my own way – with sharp steel. And then I will sit on the throne of Avantia!"

Tom gritted his teeth in despair. Jeng would rule Avantia with Kensa's Dark Magic at his side – and there was nothing Tom could do about it!

The Quest had failed.

7

THE POWER OF THE STAR

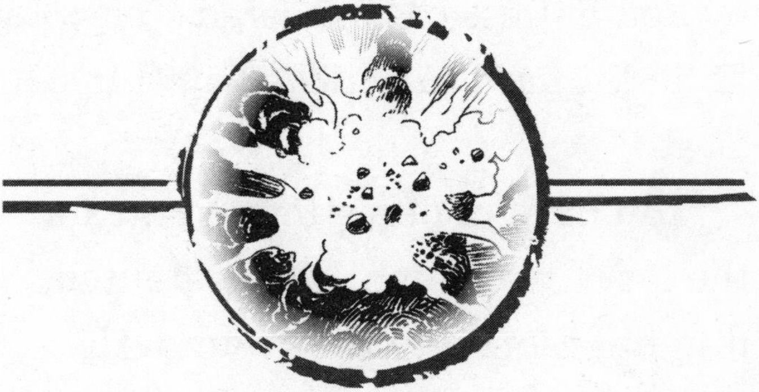

Kensa paused on the threshold of the flame-rimmed portal. Tom watched intently as she turned to look at Jeng, a suspicious expression twisting her face.

"I don't remember agreeing that *you* would sit upon the throne of Avantia," she said sharply. "I have the greater power. Perhaps I should rule – alone!"

"I think not!" snapped Jeng.

"You witless oaf," sneered Kensa. "I find it hard to believe you think at all!"

"You have underestimated me for the last time, witch!" Jeng shouted, flinging Elenna to the ground. He lunged forwards, moving as swiftly as a striking snake, even with all his bulk. Before Kensa could react, he snatched the Lightning Staff from her hands and aimed it at her chest, the Fallen Star glowing at its tip. She fell back, hissing, her eyes aflame in her furious face.

Tom tensed, waiting for his chance

to attack. Elenna was out of danger, but the Fallen Star was deadly – he had to be careful.

Jeng thrust the Lightning Staff at Kensa, forcing her backwards. "I will be your king," he growled. "Think yourself lucky if I make you my royal sorceress."

Kensa snarled, her fingers curled into claws. "And you will be lucky if I make you chief of the slop buckets!" she spat.

"Treacherous witch!" shouted Jeng.

With a ferocious cry, Kensa flung herself at Jeng, grabbing the Lightning Staff in both hands before he could fire at her.

Tom ducked as wild bolts of

power crashed through the swamp, reducing trees to pieces all around them. Elenna crawled away, keeping her head down to avoid the chaotic blasts of white fire. The terrible smell of burning filled Tom's nostrils.

I have to act now – maybe, if I'm

fast enough, I can cut the staff in two.

Tom was about to fling himself into the fight when a long, blue tongue suddenly darted down from high in the trees. It coiled around the Fallen Star and tore it from the Lightning Staff.

Saurex! Tom stared upwards. *But where?*

"No!" shrieked Kensa as the star-fuelled blasts died away.

"The Beast has the star!" shouted Jeng, staring around.

Tom stared hard. He was just able to make out the outline of Saurex towering over them.

"Kill it!" howled Kensa, aiming her staff into the air and sending coils of fire whipping through the trees. Branches cracked and fell, but the power was far less deadly now that the star was gone.

Tom raised his sword. This was his chance to strike.

He heard Saurex give a roar of

pain. One of Kensa's bolts had struck him in the face, sending him back, hissing and spitting. The star slipped from his tongue. It struck a branch, smashing into its fragments again

and tumbling down into the swamp.

Tom saw Elenna scramble to where the star had fallen. He needed to keep Jeng and Kensa busy while she retrieved the shards. He ran at his enemies. Jeng strode forwards, swinging his sword, while Kensa aimed her Lightning Staff.

Tom danced aside as Jeng's blade swept in a great arc. Jeng reset and slashed at Tom's legs. Tom jumped high, bringing his own blade down with a clang against Jeng's. He ducked as a blast of flame seared past his shoulder.

Fighting his two powerful foes at once would be hard – but if he kept moving, he should be able to hold them off until Elenna had found the star fragments.

Tom leaped high again, coming down on Jeng from above, his shield striking the emperor in the face. Kensa was weaving from side to side, trying to get a clear shot – but Jeng was in her way.

Tom leapt to spring off Jeng's shoulder, diving at Kensa with his sword whirling.

The witch stumbled and fell, splashing into the mud. Tom stood over her, his sword pointed at her head.

The gleam in her eyes warned Tom that Jeng was attacking again, and he was able to step aside just as the villain's sword whizzed past his neck.

Jeng struck again and again, driving Tom back as he parried and thrust and sprang from side to side. He fended off a smashing blow with his shield, crouching low and coming up under Jeng's guard. A flick of his sword-arm sent Jeng's blade spinning through the air.

"I yield!" cried Jeng, falling to his knees. Tom stood over the evil emperor – not trusting him, but ready to show mercy.

Something hit him across the shoulders. Kensa was on her feet, wielding the Lightning Staff like a club. A moment later, Jeng whipped a dagger from his belt and slashed at Tom's arm.

Tom let out a cry of pain as the tip of the dagger cut his flesh. He stumbled back, angry that he had been tricked by Jeng's treachery.

"You two can fight for all eternity for all I care," Kensa shouted. "I have a kingdom to conquer!" She ran for the flaming portal to Avantia.

But even as she leaped into the mouth of the portal, a host of snake-like vines came spinning down from the trees, looping around her wrist and ankles, bringing her to a sudden stop.

"No!" she screamed, writhing

helplessly as the vines tightened
and held her suspended in mid-air.

Tom watched in astonishment as
more vines came coiling in from
every side, whipping around Jeng's
arms and legs, pinning him to a
trunk.

What's happening?

Tom spun around and saw Elenna standing close by, holding up the shard of the star that had come from Saurex. She was using it to control the vines.

So that's its power!

Smiling, Elenna strode forwards, the shard like pure light in her raised hand.

"Release me, child, and you shall rule at my side," shouted Jeng.

"Don't listen to him," yelled Kensa. "Let me go free and I'll teach you all the dark sorceries at my command."

Elenna looked from one to the other, her eyes narrowing. "I don't think so," she said.

Tom continued to watch in amazement as more and more vines came alive, curling around and around the two villains until they were bound from their necks to their feet. *She's controlling the vines with her will!*

Above his head, Tom heard Saurex give a roar of approval.

Tom and Elenna looked at one another. They didn't need to speak. The Quest was over.

Gwildor – and Avantia – were safe once more!

THE WITCH OF GWILDOR

"It took several days to cross Gwildor with our prisoners," Tom said, concluding his tale of the Quest.

They were in the throne room of the royal palace in the city of Jengtor. The Good Witch Irina stood quietly to one side. Freya was on the steps that led to the throne, dressed in her armour. Her eyes flashed as Tom told his tale.

"But why didn't you use the star and the Lightning Staff to create a portal?" she asked.

Tom frowned. "No one should wield such dangerous power," he explained. "On our way here, I stopped at the northern port of Freeshor. I took a boat out onto the ocean and scattered the fragments of the star. Let them lie on the ocean's deep floor, hidden for ever."

Freya nodded. "So be it," she said.

"The other reason we were on the road so long is that our prisoners were very slow," added Elenna, with a wry smile. "They dragged their feet every step of the way!"

"I dare say they did," murmured Irina. She raised a hand and a guard opened the tall doors to the throne room. "Bring them in."

Tom heard arguing voices.

"If you had killed them when you had the chance, I'd be sitting on the throne, instead of arriving here in chains!" Jeng snarled as he and the witch were led into the room.

"If your sword arm was as strong as your breath, you'd have finished the boy off in battle," growled Kensa.

Tom stepped aside as the two villains were hauled up to the throne.

Irina eyed them thoughtfully. "So, what shall we do with you?" she asked.

"Release me at once," shouted

Jeng, stiffening his back and glaring at her. "I am the true Emperor of Gwildor. You have no authority over me."

"You are no longer emperor," Irina said quietly. "You forfeited that right when you betrayed your people. Can you defend your actions?" she asked, looking from one to the other. "I will hear you before I pass sentence."

Tom saw the bluster go out of Jeng. "I ask for mercy, Irina," he said meekly. "I only wished to defeat that upstart Hugo for the power and glory of Gwildor."

Irina didn't respond, but her eyes turned questioningly to Kensa.

The Evil Witch lifted her chin

defiantly. "Crow over us while you may, woman," she said. "Your arrogance will cost you, in the end."

Irina waved a dismissive hand. "Take them to the dungeons," she told the guards. "Let them share a cell with Sanpao."

A look of horror came over Kensa's face. "Not with the pirate!" she cried. "Anything but that – he snores like a thousand drunken pigs!"

Tom and Elenna exchanged an amused glance as Jeng and Kensa were led away, and the throne room door clanged shut on them.

Irina stepped forwards. "What happens to Gwildor now?" she

asked. "There is no monarch – who should sit upon the throne?"

Tom looked at her. "Perhaps you should rule," he suggested.

Irina threw up her hands. "No, I could not do that," she protested.

"I agree with Tom," said Freya. "You dealt with Jeng and Kensa with justice and without cruelty. You have a pure and noble heart, Irina, and the people love you." She smiled. "You are the perfect choice. And I will be always at your side, should you need my counsel."

Irina hung her head, a flush colouring her cheeks. "I will not sit on the throne," she said quietly. "But I will govern as well as my wits allow." She turned to Tom and Elenna. "And my first act as ruler will be to command a great feast in honour of the saviours of Gwildor."

Now it was Tom and Elenna's turn

to be embarrassed.

"Will you stay?" Freya asked them. "I will understand if you wish to return to Avantia straight away." She gave a wry smile. "After all, helping Gwildor almost cost you your lives!"

Tom glanced at Elenna. "Usually I would go home immediately," he said, seeing an eager hopefulness in her face. "But this time I think we've earned some rest."

"I agree," said Elenna, with a laugh. "Food and drink with good friends would make a wonderful change from all the perils of a Quest."

Tom drew his sword and raised it high. "But I make this promise

before the new ruler of Gwildor!"
he cried. "While there is blood in my
veins, your realm and Avantia will
always be allies!"

CONGRATULATIONS, YOU HAVE COMPLETED THIS QUEST!

At the end of each chapter you were
awarded a special gold coin.
The QUEST in this book was
worth an amazing 8 coins.

Look at the Beast Quest totem picture
inside the back cover of this book to
see how far you've come in your journey
to become

MASTER OF THE BEASTS.

The more books you read,
the more coins you will collect!

Do you want your own
Beast Quest Totem?
1. Cut out and collect the coin below
2. Go to the Beast Quest website
3. Download and print out your totem
4. Add your coin to the totem
www.beastquest.co.uk/totem

Don't miss the first exciting Beast Quest book in this series, GRYPH THE FEATHERED FIEND!

Read on for a sneak peek...

SANPAO'S WEAKNESS

Tom's boots rang hollowly on the stone steps as he and Elenna climbed down into the gloom beneath the Palace of Jengtor. Tom clenched his fists as he followed the spiral stairs, trying to keep his anger in check.

He'd put off this meeting for as
long as he could – ever since he and
Elenna had freed the city from the
Pirate King Sanpao. But now they
needed information, and they needed
it quickly.

Tom's torch cast flickering shadows onto the circular stairwell walls. But its acrid smoke did little to mask the stench rising to meet them – the musty reek of rats, decay and sweat.

The staircase led them down into a narrow passage lined with doorways barred with iron. From the shadows beyond the first door, Tom could hear the slow, regular hiss of breathing. He slid a heavy key from his pocket, opened the cell with an echoing clank, and stepped inside.

The light from Tom's torch licked across damp, crumbling brickwork. Dark eyes glinted back at him from the corner. Sanpao. The barrel-chested pirate was slumped in the shadows, chained by manacles to the wall. His greasy hair hung limply over his ears. Sanpao had once been known for his long, oiled ponytail – until Tom's blade sliced it off in the battle of Jengtor.

The pirate king squinted into the torchlight, then scowled. "Come to gloat, have you?" he said.

Tom heard the scuff of Elenna's boots as she entered the cell behind him. "We've come for information," she said.

Tom stepped towards the hunched pirate. "You know what Kensa and Jeng are planning," he said. "Now's the time to talk."

Sanpao looked up at Tom, his eyes

wide with mock surprise. "Oh?" he said. "So, if I spill my guts you'll let me go, will you?"

Tom glared scornfully back at the pirate.

Sanpao turned his head and spat. "No. I didn't think so. So if you don't mind closing the door behind you, I'll get back to my nap." The pirate settled himself against the slimy wall, his legs crossed at the ankles and his chin on his chest.

Tom thrust his torch close to the pirate's face. "I could *make* you talk!" he said.

Sanpao opened his eyes lazily, then let out a short bark of laugher. "You?" he said. "I've commanded the most

ruthless bunch of bloodthirsty cut-
throats in all the known kingdoms.
There's nothing you and that

scrawny lass could do that would even tickle me."

"Is that right?" Tom said, balling his fist. "If I call on the strength of my golden breastplate, I could punch you straight through that wall!"

Sanpao grinned. "Now you're talking!" he said. "It's about time I got out of this stinking latrine. I'm not fussy about using the door."

Tom closed his eyes and let his breath out slowly, forcing himself to relax. *I have to play this right...* he told himself. *The fate of Gwildor depends on it.* But it was so hard not to just wipe the smirk off Sanpao's face with his fist. The blood pounded in Tom's ears. He couldn't stop thinking about the sickness and pain his mother had been through – all because of Sanpao's evil greed. Tom felt a gentle touch on his arm, and Elenna stepped past him. She stopped before Sanpao, and ran a cool gaze over the pirate's lank hair and filthy clothes.

"You know something, Sanpao?" Elenna said. "Even if you did get out of here, you'd never catch up with Kensa. She chose Jeng over you." Elenna shrugged. "And why wouldn't she? You're just the so-called 'king' of a grubby little pirate ship with more woodworm than worthy crew. But Jeng…" Elenna spread her arms wide. "*He* can offer her a whole realm."

Tom saw Sanpao's broad chest heave. The muscles in the pirate's jaw tensed, and he sat up straight. "That stuck-up, snot-nosed swindler," Sanpao growled. "He can't very well give Kensa a realm if someone takes it off him first, can he?" Sanpao cracked his knuckles. Then he craned forwards and tapped his nose. "Which is what's going to happen, because I know what he's after!" The pirate's face spread into an ugly, black-toothed leer. "Some lousy star up in the North, that's what."

Good work, Elenna! Tom stifled the urge to grin. "We can make sure he fails," Tom said, "if you just tell us what he has planned."

Sanpao sat back. His shoulders sagged. "They never told me the details. But I do know they're after something pretty powerful." Sanpao smashed his fist down against the stone floor. "We were supposed to go together!"

Read *Gryph the Feathered Fiend* to find out what happens next!

FIGHT THE BEASTS,
FEAR THE MAGIC

Are you a BEAST QUEST mega fan?
Do you want to know about all the latest news,
competitions and books before anyone else?

Then join our Quest Club!

Visit the BEAST QUEST website
and sign up today!

www.beastquest.co.uk

Discover the new Beast Quest mobile game from

Available free on iOS and Android

  amazon.com

Guide Tom on his Quest to free the Good Beasts
of Avantia from Malvel's evil spells.

Battle the Beasts, defeat the minions,
unearth the secrets and collect
rewards as you journey through the
Kingdom of Avantia.

31901064428248

DOWNLOAD THE APP TO BEGIN
THE ADVENTURE NOW!